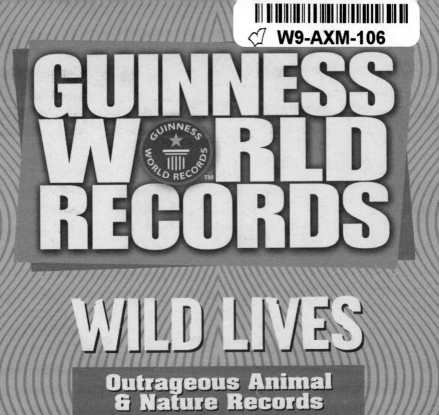

GUINNESS WORLD RECORDS

GUINNESS WORLD RECORDS™

WILD LIVES

Outrageous Animal & Nature Records

Collect and Compare with

FEARLESS FEATS

Incredible Records of
Human Achievement

GUINNESS WORLD RECORDS

WILD LIVES

Outrageous Animal & Nature Records

Compiled by Dina Anastasio and Ryan Herndon

For Guinness World Records:
Laura Barrett, Craig Glenday, Hein Le Roux,
Ben Way, Kim Lacey

SCHOLASTIC INC.
New York Toronto London Auckland Sydney
Mexico City New Delhi Hong Kong Buenos Aires

© 2005 Guinness World Records Limited, a HIT Entertainment plc company

ISBN 0-439-74585-3

Cover design by Louise Bova
Interior design by Two Red Shoes Design Inc.
Photo Research by Els Rijper
Records from the Archives of Guinness World Records

12 11 10 9 8 7 6 5 4 3 2 1   5/0 6/0 7/0 8/0 9/0

Printed in the U.S.A.

First printing, March 2005

Visit Scholastic.com for information about our books and authors online!
Guinnessworldrecords.com

Contents

A Record-Breaking History

The idea for Guinness World Records grew out of a question. In 1951, Sir Hugh Beaver, the managing director of the Guinness Brewery, wanted to know which was the fastest game bird in Europe — the golden plover or the grouse? Some people argued that it was the grouse (left). Others claimed it was the plover. A book to settle the debate did not exist until Sir Hugh discovered the knowledgeable twin brothers Norris and Ross McWhirter.

Like their father and grandfather, the McWhirter twins loved information. They were kids just like you when they started clipping interesting facts from newspapers and memorizing important dates in world history. As well as learning the names of every river, mountain range, and nation's capital, they knew the record for pole squatting (196 days in 1954), which language had only one irregular verb (Turkish), and that the grouse — flying at a timed speed of 43.5 miles per hour — is faster than the golden plover at 40.4 miles per hour.

Norris and Ross served in the Royal Navy during World War II, graduated from college, and launched their own fact-finding business called McWhirter Twins, Ltd. They were the perfect people to compile this book of records that Sir Hugh searched for yet could not find.

The first edition of *The Guinness Book of Records* was published on August 27, 1955 and since then has been published in 37 languages and more than 100 countries. In 2000, the book title changed to *Guinness World Records* and has since set an incredible record of its own: Excluding non-copyrighted books such as the Bible and the Koran, *Guinness World Records* is the bestselling book of all time!

Today, the official Keeper of the Records keeps a careful eye on each Guinness World Record, compiling and verifying the greatest the world has to offer — from the fastest and the tallest to the slowest and the smallest, with everything in between.

Is That Really Out There?

For 50 years, Guinness World Records has been collecting cool facts about the world's most amazing record-breakers. In this collection, we focus on the animal and plant kingdoms. From the friendliest to the most dangerous, the coldest to the wettest, in fossils and in flocks — the creatures and the climates of the natural world amaze and astonish us.

Out of the thousands of incredible records reviewed every year, we have selected some of the most outrageous animal and nature records to answer the question: "Is that *really* out there?"

Take a whiff of the smelliest flower, stare eye to beak with the most dangerous bird, measure the longest fangs on a snake, trek across the driest place on the planet — these are just a few of the natural wonders living and growing in the world around us.

Yes, that really *is* out there!

Chapter 1
Exploring Our World

Have you heard this famous saying: "Everyone talks about the weather, but no one ever does anything about it"? There's not much you can do about 2-pound hailstones or -90°F weather, except get inside FAST! This chapter is filled with all kinds of climate and weather records. So button your coat or get out your bathing suit, and read on.

Driest Place on Earth

How much does it rain where you live? In most deserts, it is hot and dry. There is not a lot of rain. But the Atacama Desert in northern Chile (below) is the driest of the dry. This parched land received only 0.02 inches of rainfall from 1964 to 2001. Rare storms will rain upon a tiny area of this vast desert only several times . . . a century!

Rain or Shine?

"Water, water everywhere, nor any drop to drink."

Could this be what the people in one city sing as they pole from place to place? The city of Venice, Italy, can't stop flooding. Venice is a city of water "streets." People get around by boat not car. By 1998, the squares and streets were flooded one out of every three days and every year it gets worse.

In the other extreme, it didn't rain at all in China between the years 1876 and 1879. Nine to thirteen million people died. Which climate would you prefer to live in?

Coldest Permanently Inhabited Place

Is it cold where you live? How do you deal with frigid weather? The coldest permanently inhabited place in the world is a village in Siberia, in northern Russia. The temperature in the small village of Oymyakon (above) dropped to -90°F in 1933, and an unofficial -98°F has been reported.

Greatest Temperature Range in a 24-Hour Period

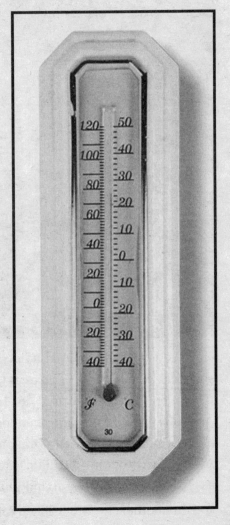

Have you ever had to cuddle under a blanket — after a hot summer day? Sometimes the temperature drops suddenly when you least expect it. It must have been quite a shock to the people of Browning, Montana, when the temperature fell 100°F in one day. It went from 44°F to -56°F between January 23 and 24, 1916!

Largest Underground Lake

Have you ever explored a cave? Most caves are damp, but some caves hide pools or lakes at the bottom. Pictured above is the Lake Cave, discovered in 1867, located near Augusta, Australia. In 1986, the largest underground lake was discovered in the Drachenhauchloch (Dragon's Breath) cave in Namibia, Africa. Surveyors in 1991 didn't find a dragon when they went exploring; instead, they found out that this underground lake was 276 feet deep, with a surface area of 6.45 acres!

Heaviest Hailstones

Hail is frozen water that drops from a cloud. Sometimes the wind blows water back up into the cold part of the cloud. More ice forms around the frozen water droplet, forming a "stone" made of ice. The more times the hail rises and falls from the cloud, the bigger the ice around the hailstone gets. Some heavy hailstones, weighing 2 pounds each (heavier than a golf ball), reportedly killed 92 people during a storm in the Gopalganj area of Bangladesh on April 14, 1986.

The longest-lasting recorded rainbow occurred on March 14, 1994. It hung around for six hours. A rainbow is really a circle, although we don't see all of it from the ground. Sometimes, if you're flying in an airplane, you can see the entire circle. Usually all we see is an arc of sunlight splitting into the colors of the spectrum: red, orange, yellow, green, blue, indigo, and violet. The colors are brought to our eyes by sunlight bouncing off raindrops, which is why we see rainbows when it rains (see photo in special color section).

Chapter 2
In Your Backyard

When was the last time you smelled a flower a mile away or happened upon a plant that grows almost three feet a day? The plant kingdom is full of weird and wacky species, like the fast-growing bamboo or the stinky corpse flower. So, as you meander through the fascinating world of weird and wonderful plants, tread carefully.

Largest Snail

   The largest known snail is the African land snail. It measures
15.5 inches from the tip of its snout to the end of its tail, which
means it's about as long as your arm. Or is it? Try measuring
your arm and see if it's as long as a snail. This wonder weighs 2
pounds and has a shell that is over 10 inches long. Snails, like
the ram's horn snails (above), are from the gastropod family.
Gastropods are classified as mollusks that have a head with
eyes, a single shell, and a large flattened "foot" – or body – for
mobility.

Oldest Living Individual Tree

Look up and wish Methuselah (above) a happy birthday! This ancient bristlecone pine tree is over 4,600 years old. This tree would have been around when the pyramids were built in Egypt. Edmond Schulman discovered the tree in the White Mountains of California and dated it in 1957. It's still standing.

Tree Hunter

You can learn a tree's age by cutting out a core sample and counting the rings (left). Each ring equals one year. What can you learn from a tree on the outside? Ron Hildebrant searches for rare trees the same way others search for buried treasure. He keeps a sharp eye out for unusually shaped trunks or odd branching, and usually measures height, diameter, or age of every tree he finds. The oldest living tree that Ron investigated was a pine tree named Prometheus from Nevada. Handheld lasers have replaced the days of endless measuring tape, but strong math and science skills, and being in good physical shape, help tree hunters continue the hunt.

Most Poisonous Common Plant

Beware the castor bean plant! Just a speck of its poison is enough to kill a person weighing 160 pounds. This deadly plant can be found in warm areas all over the world. Even though the poison from one bean can kill a person, a medicine called castor oil is made from these beans. Luckily for us, the poison in the beans does not mix with the oil extracted from the bean itself.

Fastest-Growing Plant

How much did you grow last year? How about last month? The fastest-growing plant in the world can grow up to 35 inches a day! This quick-sprouting plant is a bamboo, of which there are about 1,000 different species. Bamboo is not a shrub or a tree; rather, it is a grass and likes lots of rain to help it grow, grow, GROW!

The Green Invasion!

Beware the invasion of creeping kudzu! This weed is climbing and growing all over the place, and it's on the move, especially in sunny places like the southern part of the United States. Kudzu climbs and destroys trees, smothers and hides abandoned houses, and kills other plants (see photo in special color section).

Talking about plants that kill, check out the *Nepenthaceae* family, which eats large frogs, birds, and even rats. These are the largest carnivorous plants and live in the rain forests of Asia, in particular Borneo, Indonesia, and Malaysia.

Smelliest Flower

No need to come close to sniff the notorious "corpse flower." Discovered in 1878 growing in the Sumatran rain forests, the *Amorphophallus titanum* (right) looks beautiful with its spiked red petals and stately height, but it stinks in full bloom. The odor it releases smells like rotten flesh, and you can catch its scent a half-mile away. The bloom lasts only for about two days, attracting carrion bugs to help with pollination, and then the plant itself begins to die. Horticulturists have been able to make the plant bloom in Europe and in the United States under controlled conditions.

Mr. Green Thumb

Bernard Lavery is an extreme grower. His garden yields more than a simple handful. Check out his pumpkin (left) — what a pie it would make! Bernard holds 12 Guinness World Records, and he might not stop there. He began growing vegetables, giant plants, and fruit more than 20 years ago. He organized the first annual U.K. Giant Vegetable Championship. His favorite record is for harvesting the longest carrot at 16 feet 10 inches in 1991. Although he uses a variety of seeds chosen to produce larger-than-average results, Bernard still must be nice to Mother Nature. His advice is to keep trying, even if you have to wait until next year's crop.

Chapter 3
Creepy Crawlers

You know that song about a tiny spider washed away by the rain. What song would you sing about a spider the size of a *dinner plate*? Would the loudest insect in the whole world sing louder than you? Read on to learn more about these creatures and how some of them earned their nicknames.

Strangest Insect Defense Mechanism

The bombardier beetle (above) has a fitting name. The abdomen of this strange creature contains two chambers. When threatened, the chemicals in the chambers mix together and form a potent weapon. If the beetle's victim doesn't get out of the way, it will be bombarded by a spew of chemicals. The beetle's defensive spray can be as hot as 212°F. Its spray of gas can be turned on and off, 500 times per second!

Most Unusual Natural Defense

The Texas horned lizard (above) has armor plating, scary horns, and a body covered with spikes. Is that enough protection for this creature? Apparently not! If all else fails, this reptile also squirts toxic jets of blood from its eyes!

Name Game

Have you ever wondered how a creature gets its name? Picture the "bulldog ant" (*Myrmecia pyriformis*) found in Australia. Its mandibles, or jaws, are as tough as the ones found on the canine variety of the same name. This determined little insect won't let go once it's bitten down. The bulldog ant hangs on to its victim with long-toothed mandibles and thrusts its barbless stingers into the skin repeatedly, sometimes resulting in the death of its attacker.

Largest Spider

Can you imagine coming upon a spider the size of your dinner plate? That's what happened to members of the Pablo San Martin Expedition at Rio Cavro, Venezuela, in April 1965. This male goliath bird-eating spider had a record leg span of 11 inches. The ground of the rain forest is home for this hungry wanderer (above). Many of its favorite meals attempt to walk right on by. The spider jumps onto its prey — insect, mouse, or bird — paralyzes the victim using the venom stored in its fangs, then begins to eat.

Strongest Insect

If you think a weight lifter is strong, you should see the larger beetles of the *Scarabaeidae* family! The well-named "rhinoceros beetle" (above) looks like a tiny black rhino. This insect was tested and brought home the gold in weight lifting! The beetle has the ability to carry 850 times its own weight, which is like a human being carrying a jet plane on his or her back!

Loudest Insect

Most cicadas are loud, with chirps heard about a half-mile away. Their songs are a method of communication. The African cicada (see photo in special color section) holds the record for loudest insect. It produces a calling song with a mean pressure level of 106.7 decibels at a distance of 19.5 inches. A male cicada produces loud buzzing or shrilling sounds. More cicada facts: Some cicadas live underground for 17 years, but the majority of adult cicadas live in trees. Adult cicadas live for only 30 to 40 days, so that song doesn't last long!

Say WHAT?

How loud is a cicada? It depends where you stand. Right next to a cicada, the decibel level of its song almost equals the 110-decibel level of sitting in the front row of a rock concert!

Ready to get blown away? Swim next to a blue whale and hang on when it starts talking. Because sound does not lose its energy underwater, the blue whale's moans are louder than a jet engine!

Here are some amazing sounds of nature versus machines, in decibels.

Blue whale: 188

Military jet aircraft taking off: 120

A car going 65 miles per hour, heard from 25 feet away: 70

Bird call: 40

Chapter 4
Hiss & Snap

Do you have a frog or a lizard at home as a pet? Take another look at their relatives. Slither among these champions of the extreme: from thumb-sized lizards to a seemingly cute yet extremely dangerous frog.

Most Dangerous Frog

The brightly colored dart frog (see photo in special color section) is surprisingly easy to miss. Its tiny size (less than 2 inches long) allows it to blend into the trees and flowers. Don't pick up this little guy! This creature of South and Central America secretes one of the most poisonous substances in the world. A single drop on your skin could stop your heart from beating. For such a tiny frog, it makes enough venom to kill 10 people. Tribes in the region coat their arrowheads with the poison, hence the name "dart frog." Read on to learn more about an animal of a different species that shares a mysterious link with this amphibian.

Largest Lizard

The Komodo dragon (above), also known as the monitor lizard or ora, lives on the Indonesian islands of Komodo, Rintja, Padar, and Flores. This lizard certainly earned its status as a modern-day "dragon" by being the biggest lizard in the world. Males measure about 7 feet 5 inches long, with a weight of 130 pounds. The largest of these huge reptiles found in 1928 was a recorded 365 pounds in weight and 10 feet 2 inches in length — that's as long as your family's minivan!

Smallest Lizard

Lizards (above and right) come in all shapes and sizes. Two species of lizard are as small as your thumbnail, if your thumbnail is a half inch long. The *Sphaerodactylus parthenopion* and *Sphaerodactylus ariasae* share the Smallest Lizard record. Measuring snout-to-vent (excluding the tail), the lizards are both only 0.6 inches long.

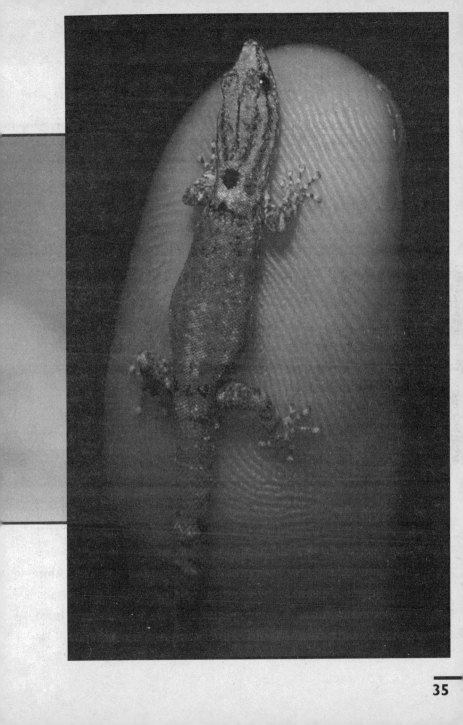

Largest Crocodilian

The largest reptile in the world is the estuarine or saltwater crocodile (pictured above and in special color section). This huge crocodile lives throughout the tropical regions of Asia and the Pacific. Four of these gigantic fellows are protected within the Bhitarkanika Wildlife Sanctuary in India. The largest crocodile recorded was 23 feet in length. However, there have been other sightings of 33-foot-long crocodiles in the wild — that's as long as a school bus!

My Pet Turtle

A chelonian is a reptile group that includes the tortoise and the turtle.

The oldest chelonian was a tortoise given by Captain Cook in the 1770s to the Tonga royal family. The family named their new pet Tui Malila and took care of him throughout the generations. In fact, Tui Malila enjoyed a very long life because his family took such good care of him. He lived to be 188 years old!

Longest Fangs

Step aside when the Gaboon viper snake of Africa appears! Chances are you won't even see it, as its coloring blends in perfectly with its rain-forest home. It doesn't move much, until it spots its prey, but then WATCH OUT! It attacks in record speed. This deadly snake has 2-inch-long fangs and produces more venom than any other snake. Because its fangs are so long, it can inject the deadly venom deeper into its victim's system. Check out its skeleton (below) for a real and safe peek at its fangs!

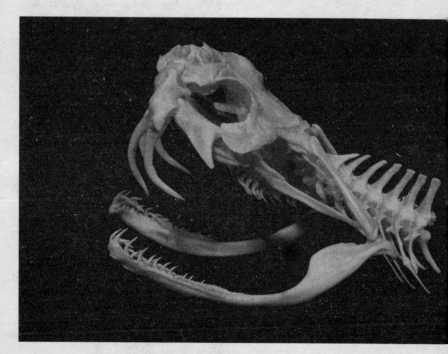

Got Snake Milk?

Snake milking is a different business than cow milking.

A wrangler carefully handles the snakes to avoid serious bites. However, the wrangler does want the snake to bite in order to secrete its venom into a handy glass.

Doctors use the venom for medicine, such as antidotes to other snakes' deadly poisons. Scientists are researching other ways for snake venom to combat diseases.

Chapter 5
For the Birds

Many birds are lovely to watch, and their songs are a pleasure to hear. Then there are those birds you need to avoid at all costs, unpleasant to look at and even worse the closer you get. Settle down on your nearest branch to learn about those not-so-nice birds, plus a few oh-so-nice facts about the ones who like to flock together.

Most Dangerous Bird

At 6 feet 6 inches tall, the Cassowary bird (right) of New Guinea and Australia is taller than the average person. Even more impressive is its kickboxing skill. This deadly bird has three toes with strong claws to grip the ground while running. It also has a 5-inch-long attack spike on each foot. When threatened, it leaps into the air and kicks out with its sharp feet. Its spike will slash any creature or person who might have foolishly gotten too close. Don't invite this bird into the ring for a boxing match!

A Poisonous Link

The most poisonous bird and frog in the world have more in common than meets the eye. Don't touch either creature! The golden poison dart frog and the hooded pitohui bird carry the same poison within their systems, and they emit these deadly toxins through their skin. Scientists continue searching for more links between these two different species. See both species in all of their frightening colors in our special color section.

The Longest Bill

Some people are sensitive about the length of their nose, but imagine having a beak longer than your own body! The Australian pelican (*Pelecanus conspicillatus*) (above) is used to being stared at because it has the longest bill, measured between 13 to 18 inches long. The sword-billed hummingbird (*Ensifera ensifera*) of the Andes, from Venezuela to Bolivia, owns the longest beak in relation to its overall body length. The beak is 4 inches long, making it longer than the bird's actual body, if you don't count the tail.

Keenest Vision of All Birds

Birds of prey hunt smaller animals. Condors, eagles, owls, hawks, and other feathered hunters of the sky rely on their amazing eyesight to spot their target before swooping down to scoop up a meal. Larger birds of prey can see an object three times farther away than a human can, unassisted. Sharpen the focus on your binoculars to see the same sights. The peregrine falcon (see photo in special color section) holds the record for having the keenest vision of all birds. When the sky is clear, this sharp-eyed bird of prey can spot a pigeon up to five miles away!

Hover Power

Most birds can only fly forward, but hummingbirds are the aerobatic wonders of the feathered set. They can fly backward, upside down, and hover in one place. These birds have extra-strong chest muscles, extra-light bones, and extra-flexible wings. As the only birds that have muscles for raising and lowering their wings, hummingbirds hover by flapping their wings first forward, then rotating their wings to flap backward.

Largest Bird Egg

This egg would never fit in a hummingbird's nest! The record for the largest egg belongs to an ostrich in China. It laid an egg in June 1997 that weighed 5 pounds 3 ounces. The shell can support an adult human sitting upon it and the volume is equal to 24 hen's eggs. Don't believe it? Take a look at the photo above, which compares the sizes of an ostrich, a chicken, and a hummingbird egg. The ostrich is the biggest bird, able to grow up to 9 feet tall. It is also the fastest-running bird, reaching speeds up to 30 miles per hour.

Smallest Bird's Nest

Flock Together

Birds fly in groups for many reasons. One bird is usually the leader, and the others faithfully follow. It's much easier to follow your neighbor when there are lots of you, and no one wants to get lost. It takes less energy to fly in flocks, as the ones behind can catch the draft off the wings from the other birds ahead of them.

What's the smallest container you can think of? Now store an egg in it. The vervain hummingbird creates nests about the size of half a walnut shell. This tiny nest builder also lays the smallest eggs. Talk about storage space!

Chapter 6
Water Works

Oceans, rivers, lakes, and ponds hold fascinating secrets, but not all of these record-holders stay in the water. There's a fish that climbs trees, and another that has the worst bite. There are many other underwater secrets to discover, and when you're done you may or may not want to get wet.

Best Tree-Climbing Fish

The saying "fish out of water" certainly does not apply to the climbing perch (not shown). This fish from South Asia relies on its special gills to breathe oxygen during its palm-tree-climbing trips. It will search until it finds the right place to settle down. The mudskipper fish can also live out of water for short periods and climb trees. Their pectoral fins give them the grip they need to hold on.

Longest Survival by a
Fish out of Water

Have you ever wondered what happens to fish when their ponds or lakes dry up? Many die, but some are able to stay alive for a long time. There are six species of lungfish (one is pictured above) that can survive for months and even years when their freshwater swamp homes dry up. Two of these species burrow into the ground, secrete a mucus cocoon around their bodies, and wait. During this time they breathe through their lungs instead of their gills.

Deepest Point in the Ocean

Have you ever wondered how deep the deepest part of the ocean is? Probably a lot farther down than you thought. In 1951, the survey ship *Challenger* identified the Marianas Trench in the Pacific Ocean as the deepest point of all the world's oceans. In 1995, an unmanned Japanese probe named *Kaiko* dropped down into the trench and confirmed the record. The depth recorded was at 35,797 feet, which is about as tall as 24 Empire State Buildings stacked one upon the other! By the way, the Empire State Building (right) itself measures 1,454 feet tall.

Best Animal Regeneration

A sponge is a lucky and clever creature. If you push a sponge through a sieve or wire mesh, it will re-form itself on the other side . . . and you'll have more than one sponge! If a sponge loses any part of its body, it simply grows a replacement. Broken-off parts of sponges even grow into new full-sized sponges! Scientists and doctors want to learn more about how this regeneration happens.

Totally Tubular, Dude!

What are sponges anyway? A real living sponge (left) doesn't look like the artificial sponge you use when cleaning the kitchen or soaking in the bathtub. A sponge is a simple creature that dwells deep in the ocean. There are many different types of sponges living around the world. Most sponges are shaped like a tube and attach one end to a rock. It eats by pumping water through itself and filtering out food particles.

Strongest Bite

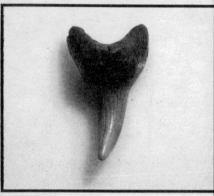

We know sharks have a strong bite, but did you know that bite pressure is measurable? At 6 feet 6.75 inches long, a dusky shark in the Bahamas can exert a force of 132 pounds of pressure between its jaws. Larger sharks, such as the great white (right), have even stronger bites. Not surprisingly, no one has been able to take their measurements just yet!

Pearly Whites

Looking for a shark tooth? No problem. Sharks have so many teeth — several rows, in fact — that they frequently lose their teeth. Yet there aren't any holes in this fish's fierce smile. As soon as a tooth from one layer falls out, one from another layer takes its place. The number of teeth in a shark's mouth varies greatly from species to species. The great white shark has 3,000 teeth!

Chapter 7
Mighty Mammals

What's a mammal anyway? You're a mammal and so is your family dog, but not your pet snake. A mammal is a warm-blooded vertebrate, an animal with a backbone. A mammal also has skin more or less covered with hair. Mammals nourish their young with milk. Let's meet more record-holders, including the long-distance winner of the mighty mammal race!

Fastest Land Mammals

The cheetah (see photo in special color section) is a sprinter, able to dominate short-distance races. The pronghorn antelope (above), on the other hand, is the long-distance runner to beat. The cheetah can maintain a steady maximum speed of 62–65 miles per hour for a while, but loses steam over the longer distances. The pronghorn keeps a steady pace of 35 miles per hour for 4 miles. So who would you pick to race?

Slowest Mammal

If you raced the three-toed sloth of South America, you would certainly win. The sloth takes its time enjoying life. It spends most of its day hanging upside down in trees ... eating and sleeping, and sleeping and eating. When the sloth drops to the ground, it won't rush to get where it's going. This sluggish creature has an average ground speed of 6–8 feet per minute. Up in the trees, however, it moves twice as fast ... but it still won't win any races. The sloth poses for still pictures — flip to our special color section for its picture.

Jump!

Which animal is the best jumper: a kangaroo or a frog? Well, it depends what you measure! "Rosie the Ribiter" from California set the world record at the annual Frog Jump in May 1986. Rosie's jump measured 21 feet and 5.75 inches in length.

Recorded leaps by kangaroos have hit the heights of 10 feet in New South Wales, Australia, back in January 1951. There have been reports of higher jumps, but no one has measured it yet!

Most Fearless Animal

The ratel, or honey badger (right), loves a good fight. This scrappy animal lives in the forest and brush country of Africa, the Middle East, and India. Visitors are not welcome. Explore too close to its home and the badger will be in your face. Neither size nor bite matters to the badger. Its skin is so tough that bee stings, porcupine quills, and snakebites don't bother it. Its skin is also loose enough to prevent a predator from gaining the upper hand. If grabbed by the scruff of its neck, the badger will turn inside its skin and bite its attacker until released.

Fight of the Century

Who would win if a wolverine went up against a badger? The wolverine has 38 sharp teeth and five sharp claws on each paw. It is sometimes called the skunk bear because it produces a strong odor. It is fierce and strong. The badger has short legs and a flat body. It, too, has long, sharp claws. It is also fierce and strong. The stink badger shoots a nasty liquid at its enemy. So who would win? Neither likes to give up, yet the smell would certainly keep other animals from getting close enough to declare a winner!

Longest Tongue

Can you imagine having a tongue that is half as long as your body? That's how long the tongue of a giant anteater is. This long-tongued mammal's body measures 3–6 feet in length and its tongue is almost 2 feet long. This strange-looking creature can eat as many as 30,000 insects a day! It just rips open a termite hill and slurps up its ongoing meal (above).

Smallest Primate

Talk to Me

We know humans are closely related to apes, but did you know that a gorilla can talk back to us? Koko was born in captivity at the San Francisco Zoo. Dr. Francine Patterson taught her American Sign Language in 1972. By 2000, Koko had a working vocabulary of more than 1,000 signs and understood roughly 2,000 words of English. She can refer to the past and future, argue, make jokes, and even tell lies! Koko is the record-holder for the gorilla most proficient in sign language – and that's the truth!

Could a monkey fit in the palm of your hand? The pygmy mouse lemur can! This animal from western Madagascar is about the size of your finger, if you don't count its long tail. This little primate's head and body measure just 2.4 inches long, but its tail is 5.4 inches long — more than twice as long as the rest of it! The pygmy mouse lemur weighs only 1.08 ounces.

Chapter 8
Perfectly Outrageous Pets

Do you have a pet, or two, or three? Is there something amazing about your animal buddy? Of course there is! Do you have a chatty parrot, or a dog with ears that dust the floor? How many tricks have you tried to teach your pet? This chapter introduces us to some perfectly outrageous best friends who like sharing their homes with us!

Tallest and Longest Dog

Is your pet taller than you? There are several big dogs, like the Newfoundland and the Saint Bernard. The Great Dane has an average height of 29.5 inches, measuring from the ground to the top of the shoulder. Harvey towers at 41.5 inches and loves to see eye to eye with his owner, Charles Dodman (above). Harvey also holds the record for longest dog by measuring 91 inches from his wet nose to the tip of his wagging tail.

Dog with the Longest Ears

Rabbits have long ears, as do some mules, but a dog with ears longer than the others? Mr. Jeffries (above) is a basset hound living in the United Kingdom with his owner, Phil Jeffries. His 11.5-inch-long ears carried the record until 2003. Now, another basset hound named Jack vom Forster Wald (pictured on the front cover) in Germany claims the title with his 13-inch-long ears! All the better for him to hear the crowds cheering for him.

New Tricks

Striker, a clever border collie, set the record for Fastest Car Window Opened by a Dog on August 14, 2003, in Quebec City, Canada. He unwound a non-electric car window in 13 seconds using his paw and nose. When teaching your dog tricks, make sure you say the command clearly, such as "sit" or "jump." Praise your dog while he is doing the trick. Then say a closing word, such as "okay" to let him know that the trick is over. Don't forget to reward him with a small treat.

Most Talkative Parrot

How many words do you know? Iris Frost found her pet, a parrot named Prudle, in Jinja, Uganda. For 35 years, Prudle used her 800-English-word vocabulary to hold polite conversations. She said "good morning" upon waking, and "good night" when she went to sleep. She croaked, "Want to come out," when she wished to take a stroll outside of her cage.

Tallest Living Horse

Sometimes you need a boost when climbing onto the back of a horse. Pull out a ladder if going for a ride on Goliath! A male black Percheron draft horse, Goliath (above) measured 77 inches tall on July 24, 2003. This giant creature eats about 50 pounds of hay and drinks about 30 gallons of water daily.

Cat with the Most Toes

Typical cats have 18 toes. Tabby cat Jake (not pictured) has a lot more toes than he knows! The official toe-counters found 28 toes during their counting session on September 24, 2002. Jake has seven toes on each of his paws. Each toe has its own claw, pad, and bone structure. Jake calls Bonfield, Canada, home with his owners, Michelle and Paul Contant.

Toe Notes

Ever count your pet's toes? If you hold on to them long enough, compare their toes with these facts about fancy feet!

• Pigs, deer, cattle, and antelope all have hoofed feet with an even number of toes.

• Horses, tapirs, and rhinoceroses have an odd number of toes.

• Dogs have four toes on their hind feet, and five on their front feet.

• Anteaters have five toes on each foot.

• Most chickens have four toes on each foot. Some, like the silky, have five.

Chapter 9
Don't Mess with Mother Nature

Hurricanes, tornadoes, earthquakes, floods, and other natural disasters are scary and life threatening. These violent outbursts on the part of Mother Nature create havoc, destroy homes, and wipe out communities. This chapter focuses on five extreme natural disasters.

Greatest Mass Extinction

Something very strange occurred about 248 million years ago. Some scientists believe an event on Earth, possibly erupting volcanoes, caused the climate to change rapidly. This sudden shift in the climate wiped out 90 percent of all marine species and 70 percent of all higher land animals.

Greatest Flood

Most floods occur after heavy rainstorms or when winter snow melts. The water in lakes and rivers overflows, and the land temporarily disappears beneath the water. The greatest flood ever recorded took place about 18,000 years ago when a lake in Siberia ruptured. The 1,600-foot-deep flood traveled at 100 miles per hour.

Deadliest Earthquake

An earthquake occurs when pieces of the earth's crust shift, releasing energy powerful enough to break the earth's outer shell. Scientists at the Southern California Earthquake Center use Global Positioning System technology (above) for monitoring these changes along the San Andreas Fault line and its hazards to urban areas like Los Angeles. Although many buildings can withstand the stresses of an earthquake and its aftershocks, a great deal of damage still occurs. The deadliest earthquake on record occurred in China on February 2, 1556. It is believed to have killed about 830,000 people.

Most Active Volcano

Lava Land

Volcanoes can give birth to islands. An underwater volcano erupts and its lava flow builds a mountain until the peak pokes above the water's surface. Look, land in the middle of the sea! Some volcano-created islands are small, barely 12 acres around. Others are large and famous, such as Hawaii.

Have you ever seen a volcano? A volcano is a mountain that sits on a pool of molten rock. When pressure builds below, volcanoes blow their stacks. A volcanic eruption spews lava and gases through the opening at the top. Today, the most active volcano is on Kilauea in Hawaii (see photo in special color section). It has been erupting since 1983, discharging lava at a rate of 176 feet per second.

Deadliest Hurricane

Hurricanes are larger powerful storms that gather energy from warm ocean waters. They lose some of their power as they pass over land. The winds and floods that come with hurricanes can destroy property and people. The deadliest hurricane hit the Ganges Delta Islands in Bangladesh between November 11 and 12, 1970. It killed about one million people.

Storm Chasers

How do you study a tornado? Professor Joshua Wurman is a professional "storm chaser." He operated the University of Oklahoma's "Doppler on Wheels" mobile weather observatory to study a tornado near Mulhall, Oklahoma, on May 3, 1999. The tornado had a diameter of around 5,250 feet. It was the largest ever measured! That same day, he recorded the fastest wind speed ever during the Bridgecreek/Moore/Oklahoma City tornado. The wind speed was between 281 and 321 miles per hour! Check out the photo to see more storm chasers videotaping another developing Oklahoma storm.

A tornado is a whirling column of air that looks like a funnel.

A cyclone is a storm in which air circulates around an "eye," or calmer area, in the center of the storm.

A hurricane is a severe tropical cyclone. It has a wind speed greater than 74 miles per hour.

A tsunami is a very large ocean wave caused by an underwater earthquake or volcanic eruption.

Chapter 10
Saving Our World

Our world is precious and most creatures — animals, plants, and people — depend on its well-being in order to survive. We know the dinosaurs are no longer around, but certain creatures even today might "go the way of the dinosaurs" and become extinct. Learn about some of the methods people use to protect animals and the land they call home, and how you can help.

Rarest Marine Mammal

The number of baiji, or Yangtze River dolphins (above), is shrinking fast. There are only a few dozen of these mammals left in the world. These wonderful creatures are killed for their meat and oil ambergris. They are also disappearing quickly due to pollution and accidental capture in the nets of fishermen.

Rarest Land Mammal

Please Don't Go!

At one time there were many large, one-horned Javan rhinos (above), but today there are only about 60 left. Fifty of these creatures live in Java, Indonesia. The other 10 live in Vietnam. Many species of rhino are disappearing because they are being poached for their horns and skin, and their habitats are being destroyed.

The International Union for the Conservation of Nature's Red List of Threatened Species issues its warning every year. For example, the blue macaw is now considered to be extinct in the wild, yet there's hope for survival in the 66 individual birds carefully protected by captivity. Zoos are not the only answer. A "Green Great Wall" is being crafted in northwest China to combat over-farming and to preserve the forests and wildlife living within its 87.9 million acres.

Largest Tropical Forest Reserve

Many people are searching for ways to protect endangered species and their natural habitats. The Tumucumaque National Park (above), in the northern Amazon state of Brazil, is one way. Tumucumaque means "rock on top of the mountain." Because this park contains many endangered plants and animals, it is the largest in the world. Its protected area covers 15,010 square miles or 9.6 million acres. That's about the size of the states of Connecticut and New Jersey put together!

Largest Tiger Litter Born in Captivity

Capturing and breeding animals to continue their lifelines is another way people are trying to help. The largest litter of tigers to be born in captivity is six. On November 18, 2003, parents Bety and Conde welcomed their new family at the Buenos Aires Zoo in Argentina. The three male and three female cubs are Bengal white tigers (above), and their birth has successfully increased the world population of this endangered species.

Rarest Species to Be Cloned

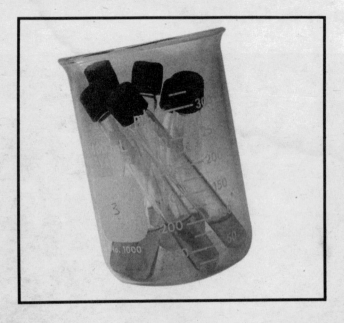

A major scientific breakthrough and the next step in conservation occurred on October 1, 2001. Scientists announced the first-ever successful cloning of an endangered species, a European Mouflon lamb. Cloning is a success when a strand of an animal's DNA is used to create a duplicate of the original animal. This rare breed of sheep lives on the islands of Cyprus, Sardinia, and Corsica. There are less than 1,000 mature Mouflon sheep surviving in the wild. A European team, led by the University of Teramo, Italy, created the clone. Previous attempts had failed. The cloned animal is now living in a wildlife center in Sardinia.

HOME PROTECTION

**Follow these tips to help preserve
a home . . . yours and theirs.**

IN THE OCEAN

- Don't touch coral reefs, or the fish or animals that live there.
- Don't touch the fish and animals that live in tide pools.
- Bag your trash and throw it away properly. Plastic can kill marine fish and animals.
- Never pour oil, grease, or other toxins into the water.

ON THE LAND

- Walk on marked trails.
- Plant trees, flowers, and shrubs, and take care of them.
- If you see trash, pick it up and dispose of it properly.
- Use recycling bins as marked.

CONSERVE ENERGY

- Turn the heat down.
- Turn off the air conditioner unless necessary.

BE A
Record-Breaker!

Message from the Official Keeper of the Records:
Record-breakers are the ultimate in one way or
another – the youngest, the oldest, the tallest, the
smallest. So how do you get to be a record-breaker?
Follow these important steps:

1. Before you attempt your record, check with us to
make sure your record is suitable and safe. Get your
parents' permission. Next, contact one of our officials
by using the record application form at *www.guin-
nessworldrecords.com.*

2. Tell us about your idea. Give us as much information as you can, including what the record is, when
you want to attempt it, where you'll be doing it, and
so on.

> **a)** We will tell you if a record already exists,
> what safety guidelines you must follow during
> your attempt to break that record, and what
> evidence we need as proof that you completed
> your attempt.

> **b)** If your idea is a brand-new record nobody

has set yet, we need to make sure it meets our requirements. If it does, then we'll write official rules and safety guidelines specific to that record idea and make sure all attempts are made in the same way.

3. Whether it is a new or existing record, we will send you the guidelines for your selected record. Once you receive these, you can make your attempt at any time. You do not need a Guinness World Record official at your attempt. But you do need to gather evidence. Find out more about the kind of evidence we need to see by visiting our website.

4. Think you've already set or broken a record? Put all of your evidence as specified by the guidelines in an envelope and mail it to us at Guinness World Records.

5. Our officials will investigate your claim fully – a process that can take up to 10 weeks, depending on the number of claims we've received, and how complex your record is.

6. If you're successful, you will receive an official certificate that says you are now a Guinness World Record-holder!

Need more info? Check out the Kids' Zone on *www.guinnessworldrecords.com* for lots more hints and tips and some top record ideas that you can try at home or at school. Good luck!

Photo Credits